THIS BOOK
BELONGS TO:
A serious, well-behaved ...

....

....

THE TALE OF
KITTY-IN-BOOTS

FREDERICK WARNE

An Imprint of Penguin Random House LLC, New York

First published 2016.
This edition first published in the United Kingdom in 2018.
This edition first published in the United States of America in 2020 by Frederick Warne,
an imprint of Penguin Random House LLC, New York.

The publisher does not have any control over and does not assume
responsibility for author or third-party websites or their content.

Text copyright © Frederick Warne & Co. Ltd, 1971–2016.
Illustrations copyright © Quentin Blake, 2016.
Peter Rabbit™ and Beatrix Potter™ Frederick Warne & Co.
Frederick Warne & Co. is the owner of all rights, copyrights and
trademarks in the Beatrix Potter character names and illustrations.

Manufactured in China.

Visit us online at www.penguinrandomhouse.com.

The Library of Congress has cataloged the previous edition
under the following Control Number: 2016298111

ISBN 9780241446232

001

The V&A, the world's leading museum of art and design, holds the largest collection
of Beatrix Potter's drawings, literary manuscripts, correspondence and photographs –
including her handwritten drafts of the text, frontispiece illustration and annotated galley
proofs for *The Tale of Kitty-in-Boots*. Since November 2006, the V&A has also held on
long-term loan the Beatrix Potter archive of Frederick Warne & Co., including the original
illustrations for *The Tale of Peter Rabbit*. Visit vam.ac.uk/beatrixpotter for more information.

THE TALE OF
KITTY-IN-BOOTS

WRITTEN BY
BEATRIX POTTER

ILLUSTRATED BY
Quentin Blake

FREDERICK WARNE

PUBLISHER'S NOTE

Frederick Warne is proud to publish this edition of *The Tale of Kitty-in-Boots*. It is a fitting celebration of the 150th anniversary of Beatrix Potter's birth.

This delightfully comic story was not published in Potter's lifetime, and this is the first time it is available as a tale in its own right. Written in a time very different to that in which we find ourselves today, this story of Kitty's hunting misadventures evokes the charm of British country living in the early twentieth century. In her classic style, Potter brings humor to her characters and reminds us that although it may be a cat's natural instinct to hunt, hunting does not always come so naturally . . . The story embodies the very same adventure and wit that lie at the heart of Beatrix Potter's other iconic tales.

We could not be more thrilled that the incomparable Quentin Blake was inspired to complete this story with his art. His distinctive, humorous illustrations perfectly complement Potter's original story, creating a brand-new classic.

ILLUSTRATOR'S NOTE

It seemed almost incredible when, early in 2015, I was sent the manuscript of a story by Beatrix Potter: one which had lain unpublished in illustrated form for 100 years and which, with the exception of a single drawing, she had never illustrated. I liked the story immediately – it's full of incident and mischief and character – and I was fascinated to think that I was being asked to draw pictures for it.

I was also struck by one or two odd coincidences. For instance, that the Miss Kitty of our story had chosen the surname of St. Quintin. That isn't the spelling that I approve of, but she was also called Q, which is the name to which, amongst family and friends, I have been answering for much of my life. And then there is Bousfield school, within a few minutes' walk of my house, where I have attended the last assembly of the year for about twenty years. Some of my pictures hang on its walls, and some are painted (by the children's parents) on the walls of the playground. On the outside wall, however, there is a picture of Peter Rabbit, because it was in a house on this site, in the Little Boltons in London, that Beatrix Potter grew up and spent her early life.

I don't think we know why she never illustrated this book. It was written in 1914, at the beginning of the First World War, when life for Beatrix Potter was difficult and no doubt farming demanded all her attention. There may also have been other reasons why she never returned to it, but I have to confess that there are times when I can't altogether resist the simple fantasy that she was keeping it for me. I hope, at least, that she would not have disapproved of what we have done – although my drawings do not look like hers, in other respects we have tried to make this look as much like a Beatrix Potter book as possible.

Quentin Blake

ONCE UPON A TIME there was
a serious, well-behaved young
black cat.

It belonged to a kind old lady who
assured me that no other cat could
compare with Kitty.

   She lived in constant fear that Kitty
might be stolen — "I hear there is a
shocking fashion for black cat-skin
muffs; wherever is Kitty gone to?
Kitty! Kitty!"

She called it "Kitty", but Kitty called
herself *"Miss Catherine St. Quintin"*.

Cheesebox called her "Q", and
Winkiepeeps called her "Squintums".
They were very common cats. The old
lady would have been shocked had she
known of the acquaintance.

And she would have been painfully
surprised had she *ever* seen Miss Kitty
in a gentleman's Norfolk jacket, and
little fur-lined boots.

4

Now most cats love the moonlight and staying out at nights; it was curious how willingly Miss Kitty went to bed.

And although the wash-house where she slept — locked in — was always very clean, upon some mornings Kitty was let out with a black chin. And on other mornings her tail seemed thicker, and she scratched.

It puzzled me. It was a long time before I guessed that there were in fact *two* black cats!

If we had been outside the wash-house one
summer night by moonlight, we might have
seen one black cat cross the yard and jump
upon the window-sill —

"You are late, Winkiepeeps," said another
black cat inside.

"Sorry, Squintums," answered the first
black cat, unfastening the outside shutter.

8

"I *object* to being called names," said
Miss Catherine, jumping gracefully out of
the window.

For this was naughty Kitty's plan — when
she wanted to go a-hunting, Winkiepeeps
opened the window and came in, to wait till
Kitty came home.

TONIGHT he stopped outside. Kitty had put
on her coat and little boots —

"Get in through the window, Winkiepeeps."

"Shan't," said Winkiepeeps defiantly.

"*What?*" said Miss Catherine, preparing to
scratch him.

Winkiepeeps changed his tone, and
began to purr and coax.

"Please, Miss Kitty, let me go
a-hunting too; Slimmy Jimmy is
doing rabbit holes, with his cousin
John Stoat-Ferret."

"Where? Where?" asked Kitty. Her cat's eyes flashed; she had once seen a rabbit in the garden.

"In the wood behind Cheesebox's house; they want to borrow your air-gun, Miss Squintums," purred Winkiepeeps. "Cheesebox wouldn't give it to them."

"*Certainly not,*" said Miss Catherine. Nevertheless, she and Winkiepeeps hurried away up the lane, towards Cheesebox's house.

13

CHEESEBOX was a stout tortoise-shell cat who lived at the edge of the wood. I do not think Cheesebox herself ever went rabbiting; she had more sense while there were rats and mice in plenty.

But she collected odds and ends for Mr. Worry Ragman, a knowing little terrier who drove about the country in a little rattling cart.

He bought rabbit skins and mole skins, rags and bones, and (oh, shocking) feathers and eggs from Cheesebox and from Winkiepeeps, and from Tommy Brock the badger and Mr. Tod the fox.

"There's your gun, Miss Q; much good it may do you! I don't hold with poaching along with dirty ferrets. Mind that —"

At this moment the gun, which Miss Kitty was loading with a pellet, went off.

Winkiepeeps fled from the house with a squall, and Cheesebox cuffed Kitty.

When Kitty came out, Winkiepeeps was nowhere to be seen. "I think Cheesebox may be right about ferrets." Miss Kitty shut the gun with a snap, and it went off again.

The gun was an air-gun, so Miss Kitty ran no risks with gun-powder. "I will mouse," said she, snapping it shut; it went off sideways.

"Was that meant for me? If you please, Sir; it's gone through the washing!" said Mrs. Tiggy-winkle.

Miss Kitty was rather flattered to be mistaken for a sportsman; she apologized to the person who came out with a bundle, curtseyed and trotted down the field.

"I suppose I must mouse," she said.

MISS KITTY stalked behind trees.

She saw a mouse, took a long aim and pulled the trigger; but the air-gun was not loaded at all, and the mouse jumped away from Miss Kitty.

Another mouse she missed, another she
durst not fire at because it was carrying
a basket; and twice she shot at sticks and
stones that were not mice at all.

"Perhaps I could shoot birds — are those
crows?" She came through a gate into a
field, and found both crows and a flock
of mountain sheep. "Mutton?" said Kitty
doubtfully, presenting her gun.

The sheep stamped their feet and began
to walk up to the odd little cat, while the
crows swooped over her head — Miss
Kitty took to her heels. "I cannot waste
pellets on rocketing birds!"

She hid at the back of a wall.

PRESENTLY there was a scuffling noise of falling stones; Kitty was all attention.

The noise moved further on.

Something poked out of a hole and whisked in again.

After several false starts, Kitty's air-gun went off and there was a squeak.

She ran forward and met — not a mouse — but a large white ferret, rubbing his head, while another brown ferret in gaiters dropped off the top of the wall and wrenched the precious air-gun out of Miss Kitty's hands, exclaiming, "Give us that! You ain't fit to carry a gun! What do you mean by goin' after my cousin Slimmy Jimmy? Give us your pellets *this minute!*"

Miss Kitty replied with a very painful scratch across both their faces. She also spat at them.

(I ONCE saw a copy-book heading to the
effect that *Evil Communications Corrupt
Good Manners*; Miss Catherine's manners
were not improved by associating with
poaching ferrets ...)

AND at home that kind old lady was giving
Winkiepeeps breakfast, and wondering why
"dear Kitty's" chin was black!

UP IN the wood, the real Kitty, sulky and spitting, followed the ferrets; she would not give them the pellets and they would not give up the gun.

We will not go into details; they took it in turn to go underground, and I believe they did bag a few young rabbits. But at last they met their match . . .

. . . Slimmy Jimmy suddenly came out of a burrow, pursued by a stout buck rabbit in a blue coat, who was prodding him violently and painfully with an umbrella.

They upset John Stoat-Ferret who was waiting outside with the net; and, before he could pick himself up, Miss Kitty had seized the gun.

The rabbit, after several violent pokes, went off, walking fast and brandishing the umbrella; the ferrets followed him; Miss Catherine also followed — at a distance.

The rabbit made no attempt to get right away; from time to time he stopped and waved the umbrella defiantly. They saw him go over a mossy tumble-down wall and disappear.

John Stoat-Ferret and his cousin Slimmy, being short-legged and in gaiters, went through a conveniently arranged tunnel under the wall. But they did not come out at the other side; they had walked into one of Mr. Tod's traps!

There we will leave them, as the rabbit did, after he had come near enough to make sure that they were fast.

Miss Catherine, rather out of breath, eyed the rabbit. He was very fat. He winked at Miss Catherine, pointed at the ferrets, made a bow, and turned to go home.

Now why could not Kitty have the sense to go home too? It is true that Winkiepeeps would have been there, so there would have been two black cats; but she might have stayed quietly at Cheesebox's until dark.

No; I fear Miss Catherine was a born poacher; nothing would serve her but she must follow that rabbit.

The rabbit at first took no notice. Then he became uneasy, and hid behind trees.

Miss Kitty could see the tips of his ears; whenever he stopped, she lifted her gun.

The rabbit opened his umbrella and set off again; it bobbitted along under the bushes like a live mushroom.

Miss Kitty followed and followed. The rabbit
led her round and round, till at length they
came back to another part of the same wall.
He shut his umbrella, waved it defiantly,
took a long jump off the top of the wall
and disappeared.

Miss Kitty — avoiding all risks of drains and tunnels — took a jump too, but not quite so long a jump as the rabbit's.

She came down FLOP in another of Mr. Tod's traps, caught by both toes across her lovely fur-lined boots.

She gave a loud caterwaul and then sat still.

Miss Kitty sat on the trap.

She sat and she sat.

She ate one mouse (raw), which was all the game in her bag.

Her toes were not really hurt, but so very very fast. Her feet went to sleep and she had pins and needles.

SHE sat there all night; her green cat's eyes peered into the dark.

Once there was a noise like a cat in the distance; could it be Winkiepeeps? Kitty mewed, but there was no answer.

It was very sad; but Miss Kitty ought not to have gone out on the sly, poaching. It served her right.

It seemed plain she would have to remain in the trap till the person who had set it let her out. And when he arrived — it was Mr. Tod the fox.

"Oho," said Mr. Tod, getting over the wall, and throwing down a rather bulging bag; "Oho? Is this the rest of the black cat-skin muff?"

Miss Kitty shivered!

"It *seems* to match," said Mr. Tod, opening the bag. It contained mole and furs of various sorts, and he drew out half of a fine thick black cat's tail!

"A complete set of furs," said Mr. Tod, edging up towards Miss Kitty.

"Gently, gently, Madam!" cried Mr. Tod, skipping over the wall. "I was only going to release you from your uncomfortable position. Allow me to push forward the catch of the —

"Oh! oh! that pellet went through my coat sleeve!"

Mr. Tod's nerves were *thoroughly* upset.

"Madam, I beg you to put that down. Allow me to unfasten the trap and pick up my bag."

"The bag?" thought Miss Kitty. "He dare not come for it; I have only five pellets left; but he does not know that."

Mr. Tod and Miss Kitty argued all day. In the evening Mr. Tod went off.

"Perhaps you may have come to your senses before morning, *Madam*!"

KITTY sat disconsolately in the trap and eyed the bag.

The bag wobbled, turned over and rolled within reach of Kitty.

"Winkiepeeps?" enquired Kitty in a horrified whisper.

"Oh, Sir, if you please, it's only me; oh please let me out; I'm nearly smothered!"

Kitty unstrapped the bag, which contained five mole skins, a brown and white fur of good quality but unpleasant smell, half a cat's tail, two young rabbits, partly eaten — and a *hedgehog*.

"Oh, Sir, I'm that grateful —"

"Ma'am; Miss Catherine St. Quintin;
you do my washing."

"Why, M'm, Miss Squintums, is it you?
Whatever is the matter?"

"I'm fast by the feet; and I'm awfully
hungry."

Mrs. Tiggy-winkle jerked up her prickles.
"You wouldn't go to eat me, M'm? Not to
mention the washing?"

"Indeed I wouldn't and couldn't,
Mrs. Tiggy-winkle; do pray help me to
get loose."

"A knave he is, M'm, that Tod. Now let me put a little stone in the hinge of the trap, and we'll try to unlace your boots."

It was a painful struggle, but at length Miss Kitty, with the loss of one toe, wriggled out, leaving her boots in the trap.

It was of less consequence, as she immediately
threw away her coat and gun —

"Never again will I poach," said Miss Kitty.

She limped home, and into the drawing-room.

THERE upon the hearth rug sat Winkiepeeps, wrapped in a shawl, with sticking plaster on his tail.

Kitty chose to look upon Winkiepeeps as the cause of her misfortunes; she rushed upon him and they fought all over the drawing-room.

FOR the rest of her days Kitty was a little lame; but it was an elegant limp; and she found quite enough occupation about the yard catching mice and rats; varied by tea-parties with respectable cats in the village, such as Ribby and Tabitha Twitchit.

But Winkiepeeps lived in the woods.